BiG thoughts for Little minds

BiG thoughts for Little minds

BiG thoughts for Little minds

BiG thoughts for Little minds

BiG thoughts for Little minds

BiG thoughts for Little minds

BiG thoughts for Little minds

A **BiG** thoughts for **Little** minds

Production

ACKNOWLEDGMENTS:

TEXT: Ivan Gouveia, based on Ephesians 6, verses 10–17, the Bible.

ILLUSTRATIONS: Leilen Basan

DESIGN: Leilen Basan, M-A Mignot

ISBN: 978-1-63264-050-5

Published by Book Barn Publishing.

Printed in China.

My

FIGHTING

Chance

BASED ON EPHESIANS 6, VERSES 10–17

Dedicated to:

_____

From:

_____

Have you ever seen a soldier or superhero on TV? He probably wore a cool suit or uniform and had some amazing weapons which protected him and enabled him to fight off the bad guys, no sweat. Right?

Guess what? I received reliable information that we can have an awesome uniform too! It is called the armor of God! Though it is invisible, it has the most powerful weapon ever created! It beats any gadgets you may have seen!

2

So, my good friends, be strong and courageous and let us put on the armor of God. This is the only armor that will truly give us the edge and the power to defeat the dark forces lurking around.

Those of us who wear this armor are not fighting against things we can see with our eyes. Instead we are fighting against the evil invisible forces which are trying to cause damage to God's kingdom. They will not surrender easily.

4

If you want to join me in standing strong and valiant in this important battle, I will let you in on the secrets of this vital equipment. There are many important parts to this armor, so pay close attention so that you don't forget anything.

First, we must put on the belt of truth. This will protect us from the lies that we may encounter along our way. We can find this truth in God's Word, which helps us to choose the right road we must take. It also lives in the still small voice inside our mind called conscience.

Next is the body armor of righteousness. This protects our heart from attitudes and feelings that could weaken our spirit. This armor will help us to remain pure and upright before God and others.

Before we go anywhere we must make sure we're wearing the boots of the gospel of peace. These will help us keep our cool in the heat of the battle. They help us march on so we can save those who need help. We will make many new friends along the way who will join us on our mission.

We must never forget the shield of faith! This will even enable us to deflect the "Fears 10,000" laser-guided missiles which our enemies will certainly fire at us. It will keep us safe and protected. We must strengthen our shield of faith daily by staying close to God and His Word.

Then there is the helmet of salvation. It is important that we always protect our minds from any bullets of temptation that may be aimed at us. Salvation grants us safe passage into the kingdom of our Lord where we will live forever as conquerors.

Last, but definitely not least, we have the awesome sword of the spirit of God. We learn how to wield this sword by remembering and following God's Word and instructions. With this sword we will destroy all evil influences we may encounter, no matter how big and scary they may seem.

Onward to battle we go! Now that we have the full gear, we can go on to conquer anything. We march on to battle, and we will win many great and mighty victories.

God is our Commander and He will go before us. He will make sure that we reach our glorious destiny victoriously.

My big thoughts!

1 Do you ever pretend you are a superhero with special powers? Which superhero is your favorite, and what special power do you think is the coolest?

2 Isn't it great to know that we can have our very own armor? How many parts of the armor that you just read about in this book can you remember?

3 Did you know that as Christians we are also soldiers or superheroes fighting against evil forces that are trying to defeat us and our friends?

4 Ask your mommy or daddy to tell you what some of the invisible forces are that fight against us, and what weapons they use to try to make us surrender, and how we can fight against them.

5 Once you finish reading this book, draw a picture of yourself wearing the full armor of God.

6 Is it difficult to choose to speak the truth instead of lying? Talk about how you feel when you know you are lying. Isn't it much better to follow your conscience and be truthful?

Think
Think
Think

7 Have you ever noticed that once you start doing the wrong things, it's very hard to go back to doing what is right? This is why it's important to always fight temptation and try to do the right thing.

8 Do you try to work things out with your friends in peace and without arguing, the way Jesus taught us to? When we follow His example of how to live, others will take notice and want to join our cause.

9 Do you keep your faith strong by staying close to God and His Word? This is important so you can be prepared to counter the fears and lies which you may find along your way.

10 Have you already asked Jesus to become your commander and Savior? This is all you need to obtain salvation. Once you do, your victory is guaranteed!

11 Do you study the Word of God faithfully? It is also important to memorize God's words and instructions to us, so that we can access their power quickly when we need it most.

12 As you probably know, a good soldier trains for battle. Ask your daddy or mommy to act out real-life situations with you where you could use the armor of God effectively.

13 Each morning when you wake up, ask God, our Commander-in-chief, for His help and battle plan for your day, and your days will be much more victorious if you do. Try it!

Think
Think
Think